Hello, Family Members,

Learning to read is one of the most important accomplishments of early childhood. **Hello Reader!** books are designed to help children become skilled readers who like to read. Beginning readers learn to read by remembering frequently used words like "the," "is," and "and"; by using phonics skills to decode new words; and by interpreting picture and text clues. These books provide both the stories children enjoy and the structure they need to read fluently and independently. Here are suggestions for helping your child *before*, *during*, and *after* reading:

Before

- Look at the cover and pictures and have your child predict what the story is about.
- Read the story to your child.
- Encourage your child to chime in with familiar words and phrases.
- Echo read with your child by reading a line first and having your child read it after you do.

During

- Have your child think about a word he or she does not recognize right away. Provide hints such as "Let's see if we know the sounds" and "Have we read other words like this one?"
- Encourage your child to use phonics skills to sound out new words.
- Provide the word for your child when more assistance is needed so that he or she does not struggle and the experience of reading with you is a positive one.
- Encourage your child to have fun by reading with a lot of expression . . . like an actor!

After

- Have your child keep lists of interesting and favorite words.
- Encourage your child to read the books over and over again. Have him or her read to brothers, sisters, grandparents, and even teddy bears. Repeated readings develop confidence in young readers.
- Talk about the stories. Ask and answer questions. Share ideas about the funniest and most interesting characters and events in the stories.

I do hope that you and your child enjoy this book.

—Francie Alexander
Reading Specialist,
Scholastic's Learning Ventures

To Brett and Drew,
the superest kids I know
—M.J.F.

To J.M. Barrie, who taught all
of us lost boys how to fly
—D.M.

ISBN: 0-439-09550-6

Library of Congress Cataloging-in-Publication Data available

12 11 10 9 8 7 6 5 4 3 2 1   00 01 02 03 04

Printed in the U.S.A.   24
First printing, January 2000

SUPERMAN'S FIRST FLIGHT

by **Michael Jan Friedman**
Illustrated by **Dean Motter**

Superman created by Jerry Siegel and Joe Shuster

Hello Reader! — Level 3

SCHOLASTIC INC. Cartwheel BOOKS®

New York Toronto London Auckland Sydney
Mexico City New Delhi Hong Kong

Superman is the greatest hero in the world.
Wherever he goes, people look up to him.

But it wasn't always that way.
As a boy named Clark Kent, he didn't
have many friends. He was often alone.

Clark felt different in a way he couldn't explain.

One day, as he was walking home from
school, Clark heard a loud screeching sound.
But he couldn't see where it was coming from.

Then, suddenly, he *could*.

Clark didn't think, he just started running.
He hadn't gotten far before he was moving
faster than a speeding automobile.

To his surprise, he could clear
tall houses with a single jump.

Somehow, he had become strong enough
to tear metal with his bare hands.

Clark didn't pay any attention to the flames.
He just reacted.

Everyone was amazed that Clark hadn't been burned in the awful explosion.

But Clark was the most amazed of all.

He was scared, too. *Very* scared.
After all, he didn't know what kind
of strange creature he had become.

That night, at his family's farmhouse, Clark told his mother and father what had happened to him.

"I'm afraid," he said.

"I ripped the door off a van without even thinking about it. And the fire never seemed to touch my skin.

"I always felt I was different," said Clark, "even before you told me I was adopted. But how is it possible that I can do these things?"

Clark's parents took him out
to the farm's big utility shed.
There, they showed him
something covered with an
old piece of canvas.

"This is the spaceship that brought you to Earth when you were a baby," said Clark's father.

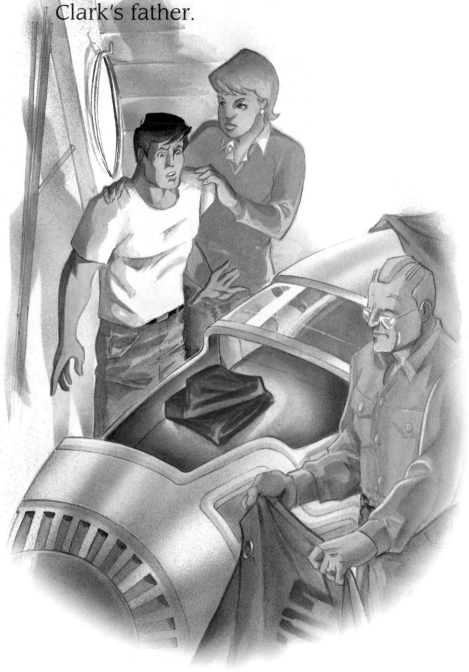

"Brought me to . . . Earth?" Clark repeated. His throat was very dry all of a sudden.

What his father said sounded crazy. How could he have come from another planet?

Suddenly, two people in strange clothes appeared. But they weren't real people. They were just light projections.

They were images of Jor-El and Lara—
his birth father and mother!

"You're not from Earth, son," they said.
"You're from the planet Krypton. That's why
you can do things that human beings can't."

Clark refused to believe what he had heard.

He ran and ran. Clark ran so hard, he
didn't realize how fast he was going.

Before he knew it, he came to a creek.
Startled, he decided to leap over it.

Then . . .

something . . .

happened!

To his amazement, Clark found
himself flying—just like a bird!

Suddenly, he wasn't scared anymore.
In fact, he was delighted.
"Look," he called to the Kents.
"Ma, Pa . . . I can *fly*!"

"It's good to be different," said Clark's mother.
"Being different can also mean being special."

"Of course," Clark's father added,
"you've always been special to *us*, son."

Before long, Clark became special to a lot of people—especially in the city of Metropolis.

That was where he became known as the one and only Superman.

He's still different,
of course—but now
he wouldn't want it
any other way!